Published by Sunbird Books, an imprint of Phoenix International Publications, Inc.
8501 West Higgins Road 34 Seymour Street Heimhuder Straße 81
Chicago, Illinois 60631 London W1H 7JE 20148 Hamburg

www.PhoenixInternational.com

Text and illustrations © 2025 Sally Anne Garland

All rights reserved. No part of this publication may be reproduced or transmitted in any form or by any means, electronic or mechanical, including photocopying, recording, or any information or storage retrieval system, without prior written permission from the publisher. Permission is never granted for commercial purposes.

This book is sold subject to the condition that it shall not, by way of trade or otherwise, be lent, resold, hired out, or otherwise circulated without the publisher's prior consent in any form or binding or cover other than that in which it is published and without similar condition being imposed on the subsequent purchaser.

Sunbird Books and the colophon are trademarks of Phoenix International Publications, Inc., and are registered in the United States.

Library of Congress Control Number: 2024945055

ISBN: 978-1-5037-7254-0 Printed in China

HEAVE HO

Written and illustrated by Sally Anne Garland

sunbird books
An imprint of PHOENIX International Publications, Inc.
Chicago • London • Hamburg • Mexico City • Sydney

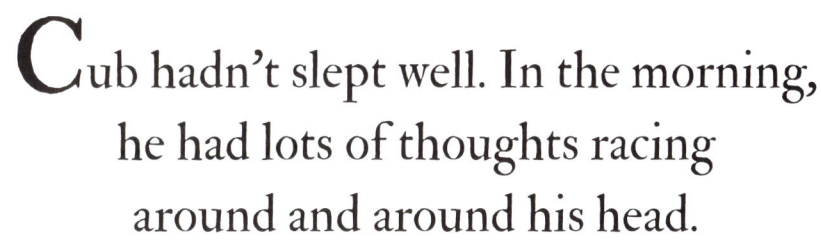

Cub hadn't slept well. In the morning, he had lots of thoughts racing around and around his head.

Cub was so full of big feelings that he had no space left inside for anything, or anyone, else.

"No!" snapped Cub when Ossie and Flick asked if they could play with the clay too.

"Go away!" Cub snarled when Rhu and Nook came over to show him a ladybug they had found.

And when little Mo gave Cub her teddy bear to cuddle, he threw it high up into the big tree. Then he stomped around and began to swing angrily on one of the tree's tough, bendy branches.

Cub felt bad for throwing Mo's teddy bear into the tree. He was mad at himself, everyone else, and everything... even the tree!

He wanted to make the branch SNAP!

But the more Cub tugged on the branch, the more it pulled him forward. The branch was going nowhere.

When he pushed hard, the branch bounced back just as hard. It was more than a match for Cub.

But instead of getting madder, Cub felt his big feelings get smaller.

Swinging on the branch made Cub feel like he was going somewhere good.

The rustling of his feet through the dirt sounded like waves hitting the shore.

Ossie and Flick saw Cub swinging on the branch and came to swing alongside him. Rhu, Mo, and Nook joined in too.

As their feet dragged forward and back, they could all hear the sound of a stormy sea getting louder.

Then Captain Cub yelled "Heave!" to his crew.
"Ho!" they all yelled back.

Cub was now in charge of a mighty ship, and a huge storm was chasing it!

"HEAVE!" Captain Cub shouted at the top of his voice, imagining the branch was an oar crashing in the waves.

"HO!" the crew sang, working together.
The leafy sails swayed as the ship sped along in the wind.

Suddenly...*trrrrrrrrrrrring!*
At the sound of the school bell, Captain Cub called,
"Land ahoy, shipmates!"

Everybody cheered when they landed safely ashore.

Abandoning ship, they hurried back to class...

...except for **Captain Cub**. He had
something important to do before he joined the others.
He quickly climbed up high in the tree's branches
and rescued little Mo's teddy bear.

The smile on Mo's face made a space inside Cub that felt as big as the sea.